# THE TASTE OF LOVE
## A SAGA OF EROTIC ENCOUNTERS

## Compiled & Edited By

### RAJEEV PATEL & VANIKA SABERWAL

Published by InkQuills Publishing House
www.inkquills.in

First Edition 2020
All Rights Reserved. Copyright © 2020

ISBN: 978-81-946962-0-9

# ACKNOWLEDGEMENT

It's not just a book that you hold in your hand, it's someone's dream. This book has been possible due to the enormous love and support that people have given to us. It was their constant support that kept us going and ensured that we would be able to deliver it on time. We would like to thank each one of you from the bottom of the heart.

We would like to express our sincere appreciation and gratitude to:

i.    Firstly, we would like to thanks our parents for belief in us. I know how tough it is to let your child fly high in the sky with the fear of what will happen if he falls.

ii.   To all the friends who supported us in their journey.

iii.  Big thanks to my publisher "InkQuills Publishing House" and Abhisar Garg for believing in our work and delivering on time.

iv.   All the Co-Authors who contributed their stories and believed us to go ahead.

v.    The readers who are about to start the book. You all gave us the power to make our words reach to thousands of people out there.

Lastly, God, who has constantly showered blessings on us.

# CONTRIBUTING WRITERS

# Ankur Chhabra

Ankur Chhabra is a graduate student in Physics who loves to stargaze, write short stories and poesies, and solve equations.

He has previously served as a poetry editor for an international e-magazine and campus editor for Panjab University's e-paper.

In 2019, he was bestowed upon by Rex Karmaveer Global Fellowship (given by iCONGO and the United Nations) for his contribution to promoting English literature and his work in Science Communication.

# PIANO KEYS

While my tips play her skin like piano keys

Her scandling lips muse my kindle

As I rhyme into her poesy and coalesce


My lips trace her being like a breeze

And satiate my thirst from her middle

While my tips play her skin like piano keys


I succumb to her tender moaning appease

Alas! From her heaven she does me swindle

As I rhyme into her poesy and coalesce


Her tongue jives around my those and these

And she plays along the tune to my fiddle

While my tips play her skin like piano keys


Her frantic dampness, my pride's expertise

Wants to solve my aching riddle

As I rhyme into her poesy and coalesce

Symphonize the other as together release

Merrily! Merrily! She scatters me like Tyndall

While my tips play her skin like piano keys

As I rhyme into her poesy and coalesce.

# THE RETURN

## I

Blank pages silently weep

And tireless desires burn,

Even the ink has now dried

But she hasn't returned.


Her touch is now a vague memory

Withholding secrets which now adjourn-

My lips forgetting her stories

And still she hasn't returned.


In a life of binary black and white,

A sea of colours do I yearn.

Vision's bleak and deteriorating

Yet she hasn't returned.


## II

I lay 'beneath the blanket dark

With million spots and crescent moon,

I feel a similar touch which sparks

The Taste of Love ~ Ankur Chhabra

A breeze of cool in this heat of June.

I open my eyes and see her there

Next to me, lying close and bare.

Her lips are soft and tender the same

Which even put deities to shame.

I kiss her and again to make her mine,

Feeling this as the birth of time!

She whispers secrets in my ear,

Of heaven, hell and everything near.

Her voice is music to my rusty strings

And with mischievous eyes she swings

Her hands, holds my pride commencing

Mouth and motion to make me king!

Then pins me down in a rush

And takes me whole in a gush.

She takes me to space and back,

To dimensions which our visions lack.

Releasing all of self, she gasps for air

And so do I, with a similar flair.

She lies atop me, panting,

Our breaths together jive and chanting

The glory of welcoming back

The Taste of Love ~ Ankur Chhabra

The life of colours that I lacked.

Now I feel rejuvenated and anew

Because she has returned,

And end my rhyme with her and imbue

Because my poetry has finally returned.

# Archana Mishra

Archana Mishra is a published author and poet.

Her short stories and poems keep appearing in various anthologies and leading dailies from time to time.

Her poetry collection 'The Dusky Dreams: साँवले सपने' explored the hidden longings and loneliness of human heart. She calls herself deeply spiritual and it can be seen in her poems and stories.

# THE SEVENTH WIFE

*Shiv and Shakti together reside in the heart of creation. Their love is not only divine, but sensually divine that has given birth to the universe. Shiva, as we all know, is worshipped in the phallic form called* **Lingam** *that is distinctively aniconic. It is a smooth cylindrical mass. Often it rests in the center of a lipped, disk-shaped object, the* **Yoni, which** *is an emblem of the goddess Shakti. This union of lingam and yoni that has brought the world into existence, is purely divine and thus, one must understand that sexual union is a pure act. Being perverted and degrading one's sexual desires only defile oneself...*

It was early eighteenth century. The story that I am going to narrate is of a Prince, then Kunwar of Udaipur. The Udaipur Palace that has now turned into a grand museum had shone for centuries with the royal family's splendour. Kunwar Rudra Pratap Singh was first in line to the throne after his father, Pratap Singh. Rudra Pratap Singh, like the typical Rajput Princes, had valour matched by none in the royal court and had even won wars for his father by his prowess and war skills. Tall with sharp physical features, he had got quite a ruggedly handsome face that radiated a strange charisma. He was certainly a cunning man, however, the semblance of dimpled innocence never made him look so. Another thing that made him different from the rest of Rajputana was, he already had six wives and a couple of concubines, a big number for any Rajput King or Prince. That he only wanted to play with so many different women would be an exaggeration because the reason for him being a Casanova is not only his desires, but his childless status even at the age of 30. Still, it can't be denied that he loved sleeping with different women every different night. Sometimes, when his passions burned to limits, he would go to more than one wife in the single night itself.

"You have been marrying different women for the last ten years, Rudra, but when will you give your father, The Maharana, an heir? You know that you are his eldest son and when you become the King, you must have a son to carry forward the lineage." His Mother, Maharani Pratistha, stung him with the same age-old question. Kunwar was certainly not pleased but chose to focus on Shivalinga Puja which he did every Monday with much fervour.

"Om Shivaya Namah… Om Shivaya Namah…" he started chanting in a deep baritone voice, offering water to the Shivalinga in between. His mother prayed in heart for her son to become father and then left from the worship place for her palace room. The whole day thereafter, Rudra Pratap Singh was in a strange restlessness. His mother's words seemed to have stirred a storm in his heart. He was hurt. He has not been able to become a father in all these years. Through all these women. Six wives he has got! SIX! But he has not got even a single child from any of them. Is he the root-cause of his childless state? Does the issue lie in him only? He wondered but was not humble enough to accept a 'Yes' in the answer. He was after all, a Kunwar! A valiant, ferocious and egoistic Kunwar!

The night had already descended and after having his dinner, Kunwar Pratap, slouched on the soft mattresses in his room, was enjoying wine. The windows were open and he was having a stupendous night view of the palace from there. The dim lights shining silently at the distance mesmerized him. He instantly craved for a woman.

"And it's Monday too." Kunwar smiled as every Monday night, he was sure to make love to any woman, preferably his wives, as his mother had the belief that doing so will bless him with a child by the grace of Lord Shiva who is worshipped every Monday. He got up from his bed and strode off to the lawn. He was thinking over which wife he should visit tonight.

"Ah! How could I just forget her like this!' He was surprised at his own absent-mindedness. In the long thread of thinking and over-thinking, he just forgot that he now had seven wives! Yes, he 'conquered' her just three days back at Nawalgarh when her father, Raja Brij Singh, offered her hand to him in marriage as part of a political alliance. Oh! How could he just forget Khyati, his seventh wife? Adjusting his attire, he swerved to her room in no time. The attendants present outside wanted to say something but could not. Rudra Pratap entered at once. Khyati, who was changing into a night dress, swirled around and grabbed the bed sheet to cover her half-naked body. She was startled at Kunwar's impertinence. However, he was smiling and staring at her with no shame at all.

"What is this, Kunwar Rudra? Is this the way to enter any woman's room?" Incisive in her rebuttal, she looked pretty much angry. Rudra Pratap, however, was unfazed by her reaction.

"You are not ANY woman, Khyati. You are now MY wife and I can come ANYTIME to your room. I don't even need YOUR permission for this." He replied plainly and came near to her. She retreated a little. Even as she wasn't looking at him, he was lost in her beauty. He had been so busy these days that he didn't even get the time to gaze at the extraordinary beauty of his seventh wife, whom the entire Palace had called the most beautiful among all his women. In the dim light shimmering through the window, he was busy admiring this ethereal beauty in front of him. Ah… Indeed, she was the most beautiful. These luscious lips. Perfectly placed eyebrows on an oval-shaped face. Big black eyes that had a strange glint. Upon these, her long hair falling freely on her bare back. Ah… Kunwar Pratap's heart raced faster. He could feel the hormones surge inside him, wanting him to crush her to his body right away. He came even closer and, in an attempt, to unclothe her completely, moved his hand to her shoulders to take the bed sheet off her body. Khyati abruptly pulled herself back. She was literally fuming by now.

"So, you want to force yourself on me, right?? Oh... So, this is the real character of Kunwar Rudra Pratap Singh!"

"The Kunwar who is hailed as the bravest and the sharpest man of the Rajput clan, is insolent with women!" She caustically hurled her words on him that changed his expression at once. Instead of lust, Rudra Pratap was now filled with anger for this woman. How dare she talk to him this way! In a fit of rage, he held her by hair and drew her closer to him. However, as soon as she grimaced with pain, he jerked her away and stomped out. He immediately called for his concubine Nayan Tara to his room who he knew was always dying to sleep with him. When she came, Rudra Pratap was gulping the leftover wine and was already full.

"Oh, I just can't believe my luck! My Lord. My Lord has summoned me after so many years... Oh. How did it happen." She spoke in a feigned accent, putting her arms around Kunwar's neck. He, however, was in no mood to talk now. Throwing her to bed, he began kissing her all over wildly. Nayan Tara took off her *angavastra* at one go as she knew that Kunwar was not going to tax himself with such a futile exercise. He instead always chose to tear the clothes of the woman he made love with! It was just the second time Nayan Tara was making love to the Prince, but she could unfailingly tell that the Prince was untamed in his passions tonight. He was rather rough and inexhausted as he entered her intensely the second time in just half an hour. He sucked on her hard breasts in a way that they were left with a mark and kissed her lips for so long and so deep that she could hardly even moan in wild pleasure. Only if Nayan Tara knew that the Prince was imagining her to be Khyati while making love to her.

~×~×~×~×~×~×~

The next day, Rudra Pratap was waiting for Khyati to come and apologize. From morning to noon, noon to evening and evening to night. He waited but she didn't come at all! Rather, she sent her attendant to the Prince to convey her message.

"Salutations to the Kunwar of Udaipur. Khyati Bai has sent me to convey her message that she has appointed new gate attendants from today." The attendant had not even finished speaking but it had already got Rudra's eyebrows raised.

"She further said that if anyone tries trespassing into her room, she will then have to bring yet another attendant from her father's palace at Nawalgarh."

Silence. A strange silence shrouded the air. The very next jiffy, however, the Prince cried in disgust.

"How arrogant of her! What does she think of herself! Is she an apsara who has come down from heaven!"

"Go and tell her that Kunwar Rudra Pratap Singh will NOT even touch her for life. She will die a virgin! She will NEVER get to live like a married woman. NEVER. This is my pledge today. Go and tell her!" Kunwar was literally trembling with rage and dasi fearing the consequence, quickly left the room. In his heart of hearts, he was sure that on knowing his decision, Khyati would run to him some night and beg him to make love to her. But no, he would not! He never would, he silently repeated! Let her live with this remorse throughout her life. The remorse of spurning the advances of her husband! Rudra Pratap couldn't sleep that whole night, dreaming of making Khyati's every night sleepless.

~×~×~×~×~×~×~

Very often we think that we have put others in limit through our words and actions, but it is just the other way round. In fact, it is only we who are put in limit by ourselves. Kunwar Pratap had thought that Khyati would repent what she did that night but it never happened. In fact, she didn't even bother to know the whereabouts of her so-called husband! It was only he who was keeping a keen eye on her day-to-day activities. The way she bonded with his other wives and everyone else in his family surprised him. She looked quite happy with them all.

"So, am I only problem for her?" Rudra Pratap asked himself one day in desperation. He was absolutely annoyed at not getting Khyati's attention at all. She should have been in trauma for what he said to her but no, she looks all hale and hearty instead. Kunwar felt even more humiliated now, much more than how he felt the night Khyati spurned his advances. He was so obsessed with his seventh wife that he just forgot all about the other six. He forgot to make love to them these days. He forgot that he wanted a child at any cost. He forgot even himself to an extent, unable to focus on his war-skills. Udaipur was already in a war-like situation with its neighboring states over the issue of Mughal sovereignty but Kunwar Rudra Pratap was absolutely clueless about his plans and army design. Sometimes he would be so frustrated that he wanted to run straight away to Khyati's room and ask her why after all was she doing this to him? She was doing? Or was it he who pledged to NEVER even touch her? Rudra Pratap would turn more vexed every time he recalled his words.

~ ✕ ~ ✕ ~ ✕ ~ ✕ ~ ✕ ~ ✕ ~

"I don't know what has happened to him but I assure you that he will soon be his old self. You know it very well that Rudra is the best in the entire kingdom." Maharani Pratishtha, in an attempt to keep Maharana's faith intact in his eldest son's credentials, was speaking fervently to him. He, however, was not convinced.

"Everything has to be proved in the practical way, Maharani. I know that Rudra is most valiant among all but look at his recent strategies against our neighbors. In fact, no strategy at all! Is this how a future king behaves? What precedent will it set for the coming generations?"

"Oh, how forgetful of me. He doesn't have an heir too. So, no fearing of the coming generations! No future generation, no fear of conduct at all. In this way, Rudra is indeed best suited for Kingship. Right, Maharani?" The aged king looked quite disappointed as he said this. The Queen kept silent. She had nothing to say as she knew that whatever Maharana spoke just now, is unfortunately, the truth. A king cannot afford to take decisions out of emotions. His kingdom is more important to him than his son. Surprisingly, Kunwar Rudra seldom seemed affected. Even as the Maharani kept urging him to prove himself to his father by handling the crisis well, he absolutely turned deaf ear to her. Lost in his own world, alone and isolated, Rudra was certainly not the old Kunwar Rudra Pratap. He had stopped shouting at servants and squandering the royal treasury on his whims. Like his other wives, Khyati too was aware of the drastic change in the Prince of Udaipur but no one consoled him. Khyati, because of unwillingness; others, because of fear.

~×~×~×~×~×~×~

Kunwar was yet again conspicuous by his absence in the royal court the next day. Maharana, as usual, looked peeved at his unfailing irresponsibility but his other sons exchanged smiles. Whatever be the reason for Kunwar's strange behaviour, it was turning to be a blessing in disguise for them!

"I beg your pardon, Maharana. But I tried my best to stop him from leaving the palace at the time of royal assembly. He said he wanted to be alone and didn't allow me to accompany him. I, however, sent a couple of soldiers behind Kunwar Rudra Pratap." Commander-in-chief Viraj explained the absence of Kunwar in the court. Maharana didn't say a word in this regard. When he was about to begin the proceedings, a sort of chaos was observed near the palace gate. The soldiers, along with some common people, seemed running about in disarray, as if something untoward had happened.

"Kunwar Rudra Pratap!" A cry came out of Maharana as he saw an unconscious Kunwar being carried inside. His body had bruises galore with stains of blood on his clothes. Everyone present there was aghast to find the ferocious Kunwar in this state. There went a delirious cry for the *Raj Vaidya* all around the palace.

"An attack on Kunwar, Maharana. By the soldiers of Bhilwara. Kunwar battled it out so bravely, our men are saying, but could not escape the stab from back." Viraj briefed the worried king who was waiting for *Raj Vaidya* to say something on the treatment.

"Grave wounds. I can obviously apply the best medicine on Kunwar's skin but it is for God to heal him and bring him out of danger." As *Raj Vaidya* spoke, everyone's heart sank. Kunwar's life is in danger? His wives began to wail.

"This is all because of you, Khyati! You have brought Kunwar to this state! You!" His third wife, who always adored him, directed a tirade at Khyati who just could not understand her words. Even before she could react, others joined in vehemently.

"Yes, it is only because of her. She has no right to be around Kunwar."

"Shedding crocodile tears is of no use now."

Khyati just could not believe it! The women whom she got along with so well are blaming her for Kunwar's wounds!

"But why? What have I done! I am also his wife! I am married to him just like you all! Why can't I be around him?" She screamed to protest but no one cared.

"Oh really! Now you have come to know that you are his wife?! Where were you for all these days? You knew very well that the Kunwar always *craved* you, yet you didn't budge! Is this what a wife does to her husband?"

"*Maa Sa,* just tell her to go away! You know right...? You know very well that only she is responsible for all this...! Please ask her to go away now!" As the wives continued clamouring, Maharani, amid painful shock, looked absolutely irked.

"Just SHUT UP! Everyone please keeps shut and leave the room! Don't you women have even a little shame?? My son is dying here and you all are busy in your useless argument!" The moment she thundered; silence enveloped the surrounding. Khyati, teary-eyed, scurried out of the room.

~×~×~×~×~×~×~

Tears refused to stop flowing. With the windows and doors of her room shut, Khyati cried her heart out.

Kunwar's bruised face would just not disappear from her sight. Oh! What has she done! She literally hated herself for the coldness she showed to Kunwar all this while. He, after all, is her husband!

"If something happens to Kunwar ji, how will I ever be able to forgive myself?" Her voice faltered as she prayed earnestly in heart for the well-being of Rudra Pratap. It was Monday and she decided to give up food and water and sit in front of the Shivalinga until she heard the news of Kunwar's safety.

"Shiva... Always worshipped by Kunwar ji. Shiva will save him. Yes." She wiped her tears and walked out. Amid palpable tensions in the palace, Khyati sat to pray to Shiva. The day came to an end but her chants *Om Shivaya Namah* reverberated around the vicinity. It was only late in the night that her dasi came running to her.

"Salutations to Khyati Bai. Kunwar ji is out of danger now. He has regained consciousness and is calling for you."

These were apparently the happiest words of Khyati's life. Miraculous words. Tears of joy welled up in her eyes. Bowing her head to Shivalinga, she immediately ran to see her husband. His other wives were clearly contemptuous of her presence but all that she cared for now was Kunwar ji's needs. As she sat next to Kunwar, everyone left the room. He was lying in bed, still fragile and injured. Khyati fumbled for the right word to say. It was Rudra who instead spoke.

"I am sorry Khyati. I am sorry." weak but firm in tenor, when Kunwar said this, Khyati invariably noticed tears in his eyes. It saddened her. She had already hurt her husband much but didn't say anything in reply. Instead, she began applying *chandan* on his bare shoulders.

"Khyati, are you still angry with me? Please forgive me. I know I was quite obnoxious that night. But. But." His voice trembled.

"I love you, Khyati. I have fallen in love with you..." As he uttered with a sigh, Khyati stopped moving her fingers on his bare skin. She wanted to pull her hand but Kunwar ji had taken it in his grip.

"Please for God's sake tell me Khyati. Are you still angry with me?? What should I do to win your trust? I will do everything you say. Please say something."

"Then you have to give me one right, Kunwar ji." Khyati answered.

"Until you fully recover, only I will take care of you. Whatsoever you need and you demand, it should be only my duty to fulfill it. I just want this right from you."

~×~×~×~×~×~×~

It was all out in the open now that Kunwar Rudra Pratap loved his seventh wife. The rash Prince has fallen in love and become calm! Khyati had sort of shifted herself to Kunwar's room as she cooked for him and even fed him with her hand. She ensured he followed his medication on time. She used to bathe him every morning and he would sit for Shivalinga Pujan with her. They would together take a stroll in the garden after dinner and often had engaging conversations. Kunwar's health had grown by leaps and bounds, thanks to Khyati's care and her round-the-clock presence. However, even as they lived in the same room, they slept separately. Rudra Pratap, surprisingly, wasn't affected by this at all. On previous occasions he would never let his woman go without going all the way but he is a changed man now. He wants Khyati, not her body.

"Thank you for your extraordinary care, Khyati. If it was not for you, I would certainly not have recovered this quickly. If I am able to focus on the work now and prove myself to the Maharana, it's only because of you. Thank you." Kunwar was effusive one night as they both walked together in the garden. Khyati, however, remained quite contained like ever.

"I have only done my duty, Kunwar ji. I really wanted to do this."

"Only duty. Was it only duty that kept you near me all these days and nights, Khyati?" He quickly countered, anticipating her to express her feelings. Khyati looked at him closely in the dim lights of the palace garden. Smooth scented breeze seemed to have hallucinated them both. She quickly turned to walk away but Kunwar caught hold of her arm. Her breathing got really fast as she stood there with eyes shut. Khyati's entire body tingled as Rudra planted a deep kiss on her neck from behind. She quickly turned back and hugged him. They remained in each other's tight embrace for long until Rudra lifted her in his arms and headed to his room. Both were too lost to think anything at the moment. The guards, attendants lowered their heads as they walked past them. Perhaps, Rudra's wives too saw this, only to turn more envious.

Once in the room, Rudra made her lie in bed and she pulled him close to her. Both looked into each other's eyes and then their lips met. They began to undress each other gently while showering kisses. In no time, their clothes were off their skin.

"I love you too, Kunwar ji. I love you." Khyati whispered as she brought his head to her bare breasts. Her fingers ran through his hair and he was using both his tongue and mouth to work on her erect nipples. Rudra would have been lost sucking her bosom forever had she not held his hand and placed it between her thighs. Khyati was at the peak of pleasure as Rudra's hand moved smoothly over her front bottom, making her more heated and aroused. Loud moans came out of her as he rubbed her sensitive spot. Their bodies, naked and entwined, made love again and again as Rudra's passions knew no bounds tonight. Every time he entered her, he could feel his soul going deep into her, igniting strange desires in his heart. He felt like putting a pause to this moment. He wanted his organ to give strokes to her insides in a way that she would forever feel the touch of this first love making.

*It is said that love makes everything possible. The same happened with Rudra and Khyati. She gave him 4 children, 3 sons and a daughter. Rudra soon became the Maharana. The saga of their love still echoes in the Zenana Mahal...*

# Daxesh Trivedi

Born in Saurashtra.

Studied in Government Gujarati Medium School.

Did graduation from M S University of Vadodara.

MBA in finance from Roffel Institute (GTU)

2018 - First Book "Yes I met Maruti".

2019 - Second Book "An MBA"

Food lover, music lover, crazy for movies & stories.

# FRAGRANCE OF LOVE

Ahmedabad

Satellite area ...

It was her 60th day in "The temple for all"

People from all faith were meditating, bowing and praying in front of three sacred symbols.

Silence was the core of the atmosphere. No one can chant, sing and speak with one another.

Manjari Desai, the administration manager of the temple was regularly observing the lady who has been coming daily, in search of fulfillment of her wish.

Manjari was serving this temple as admin manager for continuous two years.

When everyone was leaving the temple, Manjari asked her with sympathy, 'People come here for a few days and get their wish fulfilled, what is the worry of your life?

I can see on your face that something unusual you are going through...' Manjari continued.

'I am Sunaina Agnihotri, you are right, I am not coming here to demand something, in fact something happened in my life which can never be undone; therefore, I am coming here to get mental strength & peace.' Sunaina replied.

'Oh, no it's not like that, you have to keep faith in Divine, things will be settled soon,' Manjari Desai replied with positive gesture.

'I did everything, after knowing what happened to me, even you will agree that I need strength for the rest of my life as I can't see any possibility of the solution,' Sunaina replied.

'I would like to know....,' Manjari spoke but Sunaina interrupted her and said," 'I have to go now, my son must be waiting for me."

Sunaina wore blue silk saree with a white border along with matching blue- bangles and nail paint of the same shade.

Manjari wore a cream shirt with white lining on black trouser.

Next day

Same time ….

Sunaina came out of a lavish car to bow in front of the sacred and tall, three symbols — Swastik, Om and Triangle.

She wore black silk saree and dazzling earrings.

Manjari raises her hand to say hello.

They exchanged smiles.

After silent prayer, Sunaina stepped into Manjari's office.

'Sorry I had to go yesterday,' Sunaina said with a familiar smile.

'What happened to you?' Manjari asked.

'Two years ago, my husband met with an accident in the factory,' Sunaina replied.

'That's so sad, 'Manjari said and put her pen aside.

'I hope.' Manjari wanted to say something.

'Yes, he is alive,' Sunaina discontinued her sentence & replied.

'That's good,' Manjari replied with a deep breath.

"I don't know good or bad because, he lost his eyes and even memory in that accident." Sunaina said.

'Oh My God,' Manjari said.

'Would you like to have some water?' Manjari continued.

'No, it's fine, I visited every temple of Ahmadabad & met many doctors, but couldn't get my husband back, I am living with an unconscious body,' Sunaina replied with tears.

'What had doctors said about his conscience & memory,' Manjari asked.

'It's almost an impossible task to remind him everything,' A psychologist had said, 'If we can carry him to that particular moment of accident, step by step, perhaps we can get him back.'

'We had tried many times to recreate but couldn't get complete success,' Sunaina explained.

'You mean to say from present to past, till the accident scene? Manjari asked Sunaina.

'Yes,' Sunaina replied.

'We had tried this activity a number of times, he even started to remember small things but suddenly he forgets everything. If we could keep him in that time frame and scene for a longer duration, then only it's possible to get his memory back,' Sunaina continued...

'Strange! May God help you,' Manjari replied.

'What do you do here?' Sunaina asked.

'I did my MBA in Human resource management. After I left the job from a corporate company, I joined this big temple's administration team,' Manjari replied.

'My husband is also an MBA in Human resources management,' Sunaina said.

'That's good,' Manjari reacted.

'After completion of his MBA, he joined his father's firm.' Sunaina added.

'Father's firm?' Manjari asked with a broken voice.

'Yes, when his father had gone through the first heart attack,' Sunaina replied.

Manjari grabbed a glass and gulped down two glasses of water in a big swallow.

After gathering courage, she said, 'Don't tell me that your husband's name is Rajiv Malhotra.'

'Yes, do you know him?' Sunaina asked.

'We studied together, worked together and lived ....' Manjari completed an incomplete sentence.

'Oh god! What have you done to my Rajiv?' Manjari continued.

'So you are that girl who left our company after my engagement with Rajiv?' Sunaina asked.

'Rajiv told me everything, I and Rajiv are together for four and a half years but you spent nearly ten years with him, Rajiv shared everything,' Sunaina said and stood up to embrace Manjari.

Manjari could not stop the gesture, they embraced & cried....

Same day

At night, post dinner

Sunaina went to bed after dinner.

'Hey! Manjari here,' she found a text message on her phone.

'How are you?' Sunaina replied.

'How's Rajiv and all?' Manjari asked.

'Yup, all is well, just provided him dinner and came to sleep,' Sunaina replied.

'Is he able to eat properly?' Manjari asked again.

'No, he can't, I am managing it,' Sunaina sent an answer.

'Never thought to meet you in such a way and discuss like this, in fact I decided to break all contacts because of his father,' Manjari replied.

'Yup, Rajiv told me everything that my father- in- law removed you from the company by insulting you and all other things,' Sunaina replied.

Did you try to recreate the past to reach that moment of accident as you told me,' Manjari asked

'Yes, exactly in the same manner,' Sunaina replied.

'Can I try past to present, you can also call it present to future, something very interesting,' Manjari texted.

'Can't understand you,' Sunaina asked while resting on pillows under her head to chat properly.

'See, Sunaina, 'psychology' was the favorite subject of mine as well as Rajiv's.

Additionally, it's difficult to walk in reverse direction but it's far more simple to walk in forward direction, naturally we are going towards tomorrow not towards yesterday,' Manjari explained.

'Getting you, but what it is connection with Rajiv's lost memory?' Sunaina asked curiously.

'You all have tried to remind him, his moment of accident in the reverse direction (7,6,5), may I try in the regular direction (3,4,5)?' Manjari asked.

'You can go in any damn direction if you can bring my Rajiv back,' Sunaina replied.

'Ok, rest assure, I will remind him of everything, we were together for ten years. He can't forget me,' Manjari replied and spread a ray of hope in Sunaina's life.

'But he can't see as I said, He lost his eyes and consciousness both,' Sunaina replied logically.

'He can't see me, but he can smell me. There is a deep relationship between our memory and senses Sunaina. Special touch & smell, one can never forget,' Manjari replied.

Sunaina woke up from the bed and ran towards the temple, where Lord Krishna was standing along with Radha & lord Shiva sharing stories of vigyan bhairav tantra with divine mother.

'I will remain your slave for the rest of my life if you can remind him the moment of that horrible accident.' Sunaina texted Manjari with many happy emojis.

'Not only that moment of the accident, I will remind him everything, fragrance of my love and the feeling of touch,' Manjari replied with confidence.

Somehow, Sunaina managed their meeting on Sunday

Sunaina was standing in the balcony when Manjari arrived at her white Activa.

Manjari wore skin tight blue jeans and white t- shirt on it. Black sunglasses were making her more beautiful.

Sunaina opened the door, they exchanged a warm and emotional smile & hugged.

'Coffee or tea?' Sunaina asked in a nice gesture.

'Only Rajiv, that stupid Rajiv Malhotra,' Manjari replied instantly.

'Please come with me,' Sunaina took her towards the stairs to reach their bedroom.

'How much time do I have?' Manjari asked.

'Only an hour,' Sunaina replied hesitatingly.

'Fine, even you know this will not happen in a day or hour at all.' Manjari replied.

'Yes, you are confident but for me, it's a gamble,' Sunaina replied.

They reached the room.

Manjari got nervous because she will meet Rajiv after years, that too in this situation.

Do you want a body spray?' Sunaina asked.

'No, sweat only sweat, 'Manjari replied.

Sunaina opened the door & left them alone.

Sunaina was standing near the door to listen the conversation and action perhaps...

Near the balcony window, Rajiv was lying on the resting chair.

'Do you know me?' Manjari asked him.

I don't know anything, he replied.

'Not even me?' Manjari asked.

She got emotional but she managed herself.

'Who are you?' he asked.

'Leave it, do you know why these sun rays are coming on earth?' Manjari asked with an intention.

'No, can you explain?' Rajiv replied.

'To touch you stupid,' Manjari put her fingers onto Rajiv's and started the game.

'How can you touch me?' Rajiv asked with hesitation and attempted to stand up.

'The same way I was touching you many years ago,' Manjari replied.

'We touched, we kissed, we hugged, and we did many things Rajiv,' she replied.

'My son will arrive in fifteen minutes,' Sunaina texted Manjari.

'By holding his hands, Manjari took Rajiv on the bed.

'Can't understand what are you doing with me?' Rajiv asked Manjari.

'What I wanted to, with you for the rest of my life,' Manjari replied.

Her mouth was very close to Rajiv's ears.

She was continuously making naughty voices and whispered, 'Can you recall anything Rajiv?'

'What you want to remind me? Only one thing I know that I can't see anything dear,' Rajiv replied.

'You can smell Rajiv, I know,' Manjari answered and spread her hairs on Rajiv's face.

'It seems I know you,' Rajiv suddenly reacted.

Sunaina could not stop her tears.

'Not only me, every part of mine you know,' Manjari replied.

'You will have to leave now,' Sunaina texted Manjari.

Manjari opened his shirt buttons, mischievously with her teeth & kissed on his navel, her chin touched softly on his pant's clip.

'You are not that girl who has been trying this daily,' Rajiv replied with a smile.

Sunaina became more optimistic now.

'Then who am I, Rajiv?' Manjari asked with an expectation.

'I can't recall, you aren't the one who is around me since all these few years, we must have met years ago, it seems,' Rajiv replied.

'You are right, perfectly right Rajiv, tell me when we met last time? Tell me my name Rajiv, tell me.'

The game of smell & touch was going on in the right direction but suddenly Mohit (Sunaina & Rajiv's son) arrived, and they had to stop the game.

Same day, post dinner.

Sunaina went to bed after winding up all routine chores.

Rajiv was already resting on bed, Sunaina started to write something on his chest with nails.

'What are you doing?' he asked.

Sunaina went closer this time and said 'What I did today on your navel.'

'You are not that person,' he instantly replied.

Sunaina put her right hand on her own heart to say thanks to God, she closed her eyes.

This was an indication that Manjari's 'psychological game' has begun in the right direction.

'Then who am I? Who was she? Who is Rajiv? Tell me Rajiv, please tell me'

She was pleading, she was crying, more importantly she was waiting for a miracle to happen.

'Why are you asking me daily that who is Rajiv?' Rajiv asked.

'Because I need you, I want you and I love you,' Sunaina replied.

Sunaina closed her eyes and began thinking about the preparation of a next, longer meeting of Manjari & Rajiv.

Because Rajiv could differentiate the smell of sweat, could make out that Sunaina and Manjari are two different persons, despite his inability to see, despite loss of his consciousness, despite loss of memory, this power of his sensation raised her hopes high.

Next meeting place

Rajiv's farmhouse

'Manjari, you don't know what you are doing for me,' Sunaina said with emotions.

'No, I am not doing it for you, not even for myself, I am doing it for this stupid fellow, with whom I wanted to spend my whole life. How can he forget himself?' Manjari expressed her emotions with rejoice and enthusiasm.

'Three hours, you have,' Sunaina said and explained briefly about the small positive outcome of the last meeting.

Trees & plants were dancing like Rati & Kaamdev in the month of July. The place was perfect to pursue the most pleasurable act of nature.

Manjari wore red sari on that day, Sunaina wore black shirt on white cotton jeans.

Rajiv was standing near the window. The pleasant earthy scent of raindrops was soothing him. He extended his hands outside the window as slow raindrops began to fall, and he felt it, yet another sign of improvement.

'So, what do you like more? Raindrops or fragrance of the earthy scent?' Manjari arrived and asked him. She closed the door.

'Of course, the fragrance,' he replied immediately.

'Which one? Fragrance of the atmosphere or mine?' she asked.

She was very close to him and said with a temptation, 'Why did you not like when I was writing something on your chest?' Manjari asked deliberately.

'You didn't do that, you kissed on navel, a few days back, before the incident of writing on the chest,' he replied like a usual talk.

Manjari hugged him immediately.

'Yes Rajiv, how many days before that? Try to recall? Who was she who wrote on your chest? And who kissed on navel? Tell me, she asked particular questions & took him on the bed.

Perhaps a week ago you did something, and she was writing day before yesterday,' he replied.

Yes Rajiv, right, you can do it, if you can feel it then you can recall everything,' she replied and kissed him on his cheeks simultaneously.

'What do you want me to remind?' Rajiv asked.

'The moments we spent together,' she replied.

She was lying on him.

She was trying to mix both the sweats.

After a deep hug, Manjari suddenly stood up & ran away.

'Where are you going?' Rajiv asked desperately.

'Nowhere, I am here only,' Manjari replied.

'Do you want me? Want to feel me?' Manjari asked in an amazing tone.

'Yes, I want, I want you, do what you were doing,' Rajiv raised his voice a bit, showing his desperation.

'You will have to answer a few questions,' Manjari said in a sexier manner this time.

'Ask me,' Rajiv replied.

Manjari went closer to him and asked, 'What I was doing here?'

She put her fingers on his lips and asked.

Rajiv attempted to pull her, but she escaped purposefully.

"No no, no, na na na", she was laughing.

Answer my questions then I will come to you,' she continued.

Rajiv was nervous, he was stimulated. Some kind of pressure mounted on his mind to recall something.

He started to snatch the bedsheet and said,' Don't play with me, come here, I want to taste you, I want to smell you, I want to feel you.'

'Did we do something like this earlier? Tell me Rajiv,' Manjari asked.

I don't know but every sense of mine wants you to do what you were doing just now.' Rajiv replied with tears in his eyes.

Then, tell me, what is it?' Manjari asked again and started to play with his lips through her fingers.

'I don't know what the name it has but I want it.'

'You know it Rajiv,' she replied and raised her voice.

'We did it many times,' she continued.

'Ok, I am leaving the room finally,' Manjari's half sentence was completed by Rajiv——

'Kiss, I want to kiss you,' Rajiv said.

Manjari ran towards Rajiv & completed his wish, they were rhapsodizing in a lip- lock.

Manjari kissed him on his lips, cheeks, chest and she went on and on…

'How can you forget it? Stupid, you can't,' Manjari said and she burst in tears.

One more time, Manjari left the bed in the same manner.

Rajiv was desperate again.

Manjari said, 'You will have to answer my questions, if you want me.'

'Which questions?' Rajiv asked.

'Why had you broken your bed when we met last time, which is the most amazing gift of nature? You will have to answer everything Rajiv and you will have to recall everything,' Manjari replied and left the room. She left Rajiv unsatisfied and satisfied Sunaina.

Same day night

Sunaina was playing with Rajiv's lips,

She wore a silk nightgown.

'So, you know what kiss means?' Sunaina asked Rajiv with a naughty smile.

'Yes, where is she, 'he asked.

'Can't you remember who am I? We also kissed many times,' she asked and started to work on the mission.

'But the feeling is different,' Rajiv replied.

'Feeling or fragrance?' Sunaina asked with erotic coma & full-stop.

She went more close to Rajiv.

She put her bosom on Rajiv's face.

If you can differentiate between me & her, it means you can remember the past' Sunaina replied.

'What you want to remind me?' Rajiv asked.

'I want to remind you, how we gave birth to our son Mohit,' she replied emotionally.

'Tell me what happened that day Rajiv? How the accident took place?' she continued.

'Which accident?' Rajiv counter questioned.

He was nervous.

Sunaina preferred to make him sleep and stopped the conversation.

A week later

Night 8 pm

Farmhouse

Sunaina was waiting for Manjari.

Everything she managed.

Sunaina said, 'Perhaps this is the last time, till morning you can see and talk to your ex. Perhaps I can't manage it again.'

'I understand Sunaina, but you can see the results,' Manjari argued for the first time.

'You know if Rajiv's father will learn that I am managing his meetings with you, he will destroy everything, he hates you,' she explained.

'We have one whole night, we can remind him of everything,' she replied positively.

Manjari entered the room where Rajiv was. She wore red kurti on white jeans.

'So, Rajiv, how are you?' she asked and sat on his lap.

'So, you are that girl?' Rajiv responded after a pause of five minutes.

'Name?' Manjari asked.

'I know you through your fragrance only,' he replied.

'But you know me, Rajiv,' she replied.

'Ok, let me start from the beginning,' she said & stood up.

Rajiv was walking slowly and trying to move towards her.

After two wrong attempts, he was very close to her.

Manjari ran towards him and embraced him tightly.

'What is this Rajiv?' Manjari asked.

Rajiv remained silent.

'Tell me, otherwise I am going,' she replied and started to push him slowly.

'Hug, it's known as hugging,' Rajiv replied.

Only rarely it happens.

Rajiv & Manjari were enjoying the hug but person who was more happy was standing outside.

'Do you know when did it happened between us for the first time?' Manjari asked.

'No,' he replied.

'Last time?' she asked.

'Perhaps, yes I know,' Rajiv began to ask something to his mind.

Manjari hugged him more passionately...

She put her fingers on Rajiv's back pockets.

'You can remember it Rajiv' Manjari replied with tears.

'If you can remember only this one moment then you can remember series of moments my love' Manjari replied.

'My love' Rajiv replied with a wise smile.

Manjari was thinking on it.

'My love,' Rajiv said again.

Sunaina was more curious and excited now.

'Yes, my love,' she replied.

'We spoke this phrase more than ten times when we met last time,' Rajiv suddenly replied.

Manjari was shocked, Sunaina too. Even Manjari forgot it but Rajeev could recall.

Manjari immediately managed herself. And grabbed the moment to capitalize it.

She took him on bed. With the word, 'My love.'

'What happened after that?' Manjari asked.

'After that we never met, Manjari,' he replied taking her name.

'Yes, Rajiv yes, I am Manjari, your Manjari, your love, 'she replied and burst into tears.

'Not your love, my love,' he replied.

'Yes, what happened the next day?

After our last meeting? 'Manjari asked.

'Many flowers, many people, dance, DJ,' Rajiv could recollect the things.

'That is known as marriage, you stupid' Manjari replied with an emotional anger.

'My love, not stupid,' Rajiv said with a broad smile.

'With whom?' Manjari asked in sequence.

'With a girl who was playing with my lips, a few days back, she is ...' Rajiv was thinking & confused.

'Flowers, people, DJ, dance and...?' Manjari asked & stopped.

'And?' Rajiv asked.

'Car, marriage car. There must be a car with all these things' Manjari said.

'Yes, a car was there, but ….?' Rajiv seemed confused again.

'What was written on it? Rajiv weds ???' Manjari continued asking.

'Sunaina, where is she?' Rajiv finally responded; he was on the way to recall everything.

'She is with Mohit' Manjari took a big step.

'Mohit?' Rajiv asked.

He was missing the plot. Manjari observed his nervousness...

She opened his zip. And started to kiss him …

'Where did you go after the marriage? You & Sunaina? Honeymoon? Post marriage,' Manjari prepared a plot to reach Mohit's birth.

'I can't remember it. Manjari, I can't' Rajiv replied with nervousness.

Sunaina threw roses on the bed, Manjari grabbed and put it near Rajiv's face.

Rajiv suddenly shouted, 'Where is rosy? 'Where is my son?'

'Rosy?' Manjari raised her eyebrows.

'My son Mohit, is he fine? We called him rosy with love' Rajiv replied.

Manjari & Sunaina's rejoice reached on top of the floor...

'What happened after his first birthday?' Manjari asked.

Sunaina was praying to God with her eyes closed…

'Papa insulted you and thrown you out of the company,' Rajiv said.

'Not past stupid, I am asking you what happened after Mohit's first birthday party?' Manjari asked.

'Business dealings, tender, I can't remember it …'Rajiv started to jump and shout …

Now Sunaina got nervous, because till this moment she knew everything.

'Yes, Rajiv yes, what happened in that tour? Sunaina arrived and asked

'You went to Bangalore to submit government tender papers.'

Rajiv stood up and hugged Sunaina.

'We grabbed it but could not work on it after your accident.' Sunaina said

'I can't remember it,' Rajiv shouted, he was nervous, he was furious.

Manjari suddenly intervene then and asked, 'Who grabbed it after his accident?'

'Mr. Mulchandani's company, Matangi Associates…, Sunaina replied.

'He called and threatened me, the day we got tender approval.' Rajiv said

'Exactly when?' Sunaina and Manjari asked together.

'The day before my accident' Rajiv spoke with complete consciousness.

My car number is xyz 3636

My mobile number is 7664421778

My wife is Sunaina.

Mohit is my son, when we first time enjoyed sex, we used rose flavour condom, so we call him rosy, Manjari was everything to me. Papa didn't allow us to marry, and she left our organization after Papa insulted her last time and I met her the day before our marriage.

'Next day to the threat?' Sunaina asked.

'When I visited our production plant first someone threw acid in my eyes,' Rajiv continued.

'What? 'Sunaina could not handle herself, she fell down.

'Then accident?' Manjari handled her and asked.

'Accident took place after acid had snatched my vision, heavy machinery suddenly collapsed on my head,' Rajiv explained.

'With whom did you visit the plant?' Manjari made a point.

'With our production head,' Rajiv said.

'Mr. Dhansukh Patel' Sunaina added with a broken voice.

'Is he working with your organization now?' Manjari asked to make things more clear.

'After a year, he left and joined Mulchandani's company' Matangi Associates...' Sunaina said

'That's the point, he joined them after a year because no one can suspect him.

'Ha ha ha ha' Rajiv said and started to laugh loudly.

After a continuous laughter of around seven minutes, he started crying ... After a few minutes he was laughing & crying both.

Two extreme emotions he was enjoying together.

Sunaina & Manjari walked towards him & hugged him.

'After that what happened, Mr. Rajiv Malhotra?' Sunaina Agnihotri asked.

'Fragrance of love' Manjari Desai replied with an adorable smile ...

They all started to laugh.

# Jashraj Panigrahy

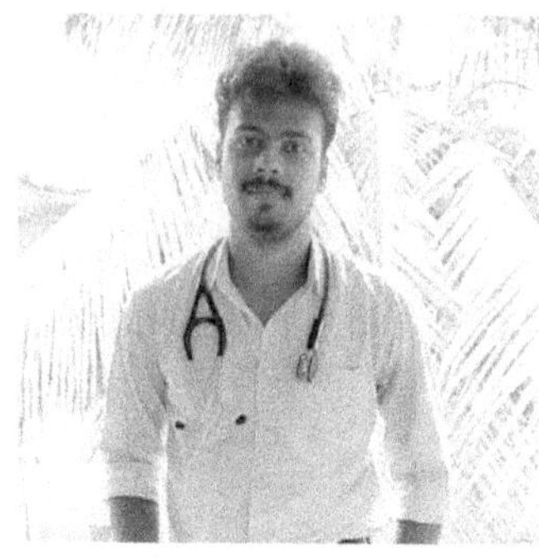

Jashraj Panigrahy is a young budding creative writer and budding Dental Surgeon from Bhubaneswar, Odisha.

He is currently pursuing his graduation in Bachelor of Dental Surgery (BDS) from Utkal university, Odisha.

He has been consistent towards writing and believes that there's always something to be grateful for.

In his leisure time he likes to wander new places.

He wishes to make the world a happy and better place.

# LOVE AND INTIMACY

A true love story is like a fairy tale.

Everyone dreams of it, but only a few actually live it.

It was Sunday morning and the weather was cold outside. It began to rain as we stepped outside the balcony of our bedroom. I wanted to go back inside.

"You will get wet" I said kissing her forehead. She smiled and dragged me with her. I laughed as our heads bent against the cold raindrops. We were like happy, carefree couples. Then I stopped and turned around kissed her in the middle of her romantic talks and fantasies.

"You are so crazy" she whispered in my ears as she wanted something more. Her lips were warm against mine. Her tongue probed my mouth and stirred me awake in the cold. For a moment I paused and looked into her beautiful eyes and then I bent my head and kissed her again, hungrily this time. I rubbed her nipples through her wet clothes as I plundered her mouth.

"Sara, you are driving me out of my mind" I whispered in her ears.

"Rohan, I need you know, let's go in "she said and laid down on the bed.

The rain falling down the window pane and the hearth made it relax and soothing.

I gave a glance at her, a beautiful innocent girl lying beside me happily. She knew she was beautiful since everyone mentioned it to her. We were buddies since first year of our college and after that we came into relationship when I gathered the courage to express my love. A woman's beauty is not in the clothes, not in its shape or hairstyle, beauty lies in her eyes because it's the gateway to her heart, where love lives. Her eyes speak a lot of things about her love hatred sacrifice and all but whenever she's around me, she forgets everything and used to relax on my chest making her warm.

She has the most beautiful face. Her lips were pink. I looked at her intently asking myself how did I end up with this beautiful girl. This time, I gave a peck on the lips so gentle. The fragrance of her body aroused me.

"I am ready, are you?", She said and this totally turned me on. We kissed and kissed and smooched so deeply. I could feel her lips on me, it was so sensual that its feeling still arouses me. Then I began undressing her. I removed the top button of her red pink floral shirt which looked lovely on her. She always knew the floral dress would turn me on and that very day she wore the same floral dress I present on her last birthday. She was looking pretty and gorgeous. She wasn't wearing anything underneath, so her breasts instantly popped out of her tight dress as I pulled it down. Her breasts looked perfect. It seemed like word perfection itself arose from her. Boobs are magic as people say and yes, they do reduce stress. Her boobs were perfectly bell shaped with a little side set as I had ever wished in my dreams. Her nipples felt like ripe berries rolling between my fingers, I made my way to the hard nipples sucking, squeezing them alternatively. I pinched them and took them in my mouth, biting them until she gasped. I licked the space between her tits. At that time, I could feel her breath growing faster and my heart pounded like crazy. I pulled her on top of me and kissed her tits. She sighed in pleasure and leaned down to kiss my neck and chest. She ran her fingers over my chest going down the abs.

My breath was able to be felt by her as my abs went up and down. Running the fingers from the navel she unzipped my pants and cupped my pubic area. She slowly pulled my underwear down and my erection came springing. She took the base of my penis in her hand.

Lovingly, she grabbed the hardness and started slowly moving her hand up and down, and She went even closer until her mouth touched the head of my penis. The sensuality of the situation was over the roof. There she was, playing with my manhood and took the tip of my erection into her mouth. She sucked on the head, then licked from base to tip, wetting my hard penis with her saliva. She jerked my erection and with Her right hand played with my balls before taking each one into her mouth, massaging and stroking with her tongue. Her mouth was filled with pre-cum as she repeatedly played with my penis in her mouth.

She licked my manhood from the bottom up and then worked her tongue in circles as she went to the very tip. I groaned in pleasure, gathering her hair in my hand, so I could see her face. I enjoyed watching her do this. Her sucking gradually became faster, and she knew I would blow my load anytime. I soon halted and rolled her over the bed.

I slid down her dress down to her ankles and went down effortlessly to her navel, sucking her navel gave her the immense pleasure. Down She was cleanly shaved, and she tasted delightful, too. I slowly touched her vulva. Her vagina was soaking wet. She sighed and gasped as I swirled my finger in little circles around her clit. Her legs shook. I rubbed my finger up and down her slit. Her hips thrust up toward my hand. I easily slid two fingers inside her wet, hot vagina. She groaned with pleasure as I thrust with my fingers. Then she took my penis in her hand and rubbed it up and down her wet slit. I moved her hand and thrust deeply into her tight, soaking wet vagina. She moaned so deeply.

She loved the feeling of me inside her.  As I continued to dive between her legs, her moaning was getting higher. At this point I held her back against the wall with one leg up against my arm, while I pumped harder and harder. She loved the way we changed our positions. We had always planned of doing in every position possible. Her favorite was cow girl. Then She put her hands flat on my chest and sat up, giving me a stunning view of her body. She was humping sensually on top of me while I was rubbing her clitoris. Her bottom looked mighty fine and her breasts wiggled in all its gorgeousness. She swung her hips faster and harder. I looked down and saw my hard penis, shiny and wet with her juices, disappearing into her dripping pink lips. The sight of her tits bouncing was too tempting that I reached out and massaged them with my hands, twisting her nipples until she cried out. The sound of our bodies clashing while I was thrusting so deep was the best. She made sounds that were too sensual. I was also moaning so deep as I was about to ejaculate. After a few seconds, my body uncontrollably shook while my load burst inside her lovely juicy vagina. It was certainly the most memorable pleasure ever. The thought of it even today gives me goosebumps.

Relationship is all about love and intimacy. That day we lived to are fullest and took the relationship to a whole new level. I grabbed her shoulders and gave her a passionate kiss on the lips as we both dozed off to dreamland again.

# Khushboo Vasava

Khushboo Vasava, pen name (theinkedfeelings), an amateur writer of 26, hails from Gandhidham-Kachchh, Gujarat.

Basically, by profession she belongs to the teaching field. She loves to write quotes, short topics, poems and even to explore new things which enhances knowledge of different aspects. She also loves reading novels, listening to music and is fond of collection of books. Has a collection of good authors like John Green, Paul Coelho, Durjoy Dutta and Chetan Bhagat, and is also a foodie too.

Writing as a hobby, helped her to drizzle emotions, which shines on the paper. She has done post-graduation in commerce field and also done B.Ed. along with a Certificate in Guidance (CIG) from IGNOU. On Workfront, presently worked as a PRT teacher in GSEB affiliated school in Gandhidham.

Follow her on social media.

Instagram: @the.inkedfeelings

Facebook: Khushboo Vasava.

Also, can follow her on YourQuote app and Mirakee app: - @theinked_feelings (Khushboo Vasava).

WhatsApp No.: 9426250914

# BREATH OF LOVE

She was like,

A mystery in the dark;

Taking off her clothes,

Shedding away every single worry,

Which haunted her.


His body touched;

Every part of hers,

He longs to be as juicy,

As a passion fruit;


On her tongue,

His fingers intertwined;

In her hair,

His subtle voice;

Deep and husky,

Whispering down her ears;

Awakening her soul.


Both mingled,

Got drenched in,

Almost smoky and seasoned;

In that lush of nectar.

Where the shy moonbeams scarce,

Dared to light their bliss;

The hidden glow-worms kindled,

As sporting, with their passion,

Low and deep.


That night;

Was an intimacy evident,

Startling a rustic adventure.

The next morning,

When she woke up,

She could feel,

The warm fragrance,

Of his shirt,

Wrapped around her skin;

For they had strapped together,

Seemed like a dream.


Freshly fucked; lying on the couch,

Deep down her heart;

She could feel,

His throbbing heartbeat.

His fingertips tickling, all over;

As if they were,

Playing on her soft skin;

Just like, smacking a cream.


His hands reaching places,

With his back arched;

And their eyes closed,

She had goosebumps;

Like crazy.

But it was not over yet,

Because once again,

This love was,

In the making…

# Neha Mahapatra

Neha Mahapatra here from Bhubaneswar Odisha.

She has completed her secondary exam in the year 2019 and then took an admission in diploma civil branch.

I am a published writer. Writing is my passion for last 2 years. I express myself through mine writings. I had always enjoyed writing as, when nobody was there pen and paper were mine best friend.

Contact info:

Instagram: @_.n_e_h_u._

Email Id: neha.mahapatra7978@gmail.com

# DARK BEAUTIFUL MOMENTS

Small droplets running all over my body. Rain was inviting me to feel the warm breath, though I was missing winter and those dark moments.

I remembered once in a cloudy weather he came up to me and said, "today it's going to rain" and then with an evil smile he added, "darling it will be our first rain romance". He pulled me closer from my waist and while opening my hair coming close to me, he gently kissed my forehead. And then with a thunderstruck it started to rain with that power cut. I was so scared at that time, I hugged him badly. We were never so close to each other. Then with a couple of seconds, we both were enjoying the rain. His eyes were drowned in mine. His body dripping wet, we did make love high with soft touches and wet kisses. He made me lose my mind, as he made me drip with desire. His body in the rhythm to some unknown tunes and drops of water running and feeling every ounce of him. Every part of his body was inviting me to be his forever. After a while I started sneezing and I spoiled that blissful moment. He took me to the room and there he wiped my hair. He then asked me to take a hot shower. While he was handing me the towel, 1 pulled him inside and turned on the shower. Then step by step he undressed me and started to shampoo my hair gently, massaging my scalp he kissed my neck. Then I poured shampoo in his hair and gave him a good time. After a quick wash, he suddenly pulled me closer and whispered, "Position can drive you crazy but we will make one ours". Then I replied, "Just stay inside me, so that I can feel the pain that satisfies my soul". Then slowly he rolled his fingers above my navel, reaching and reaching down. I did spread myself wider. I could feel his cock a bar of heat inside my honey pot, deep inside. I took him in my mouth not because I had to, but because I wanted to. It was for the first time I did taste him, smelled him, felt him. I needed to have him inside me in every possible way. He tasted so good. He groaned, his hands were moving along the back of my thighs and I started moaning as he got on his knees and pushed me against the wall, he accessed my every need. His juicy lips, his wet hair was making me lose control. Then he whispered, "Pain in sex is pleasure darling and there is a dessert to be found, those vanilla cupcakes round with cherries need to be tasted". Then he wrapped me in the white towel, took me to the room and made me rest in his lap. His hands between my legs squeezing my thighs going deep for rest. Later the towel was resting on the floor, watching the "darkroom stories". His finger, his lips all over my skin. He held my cups in his hand and buried his face on those, aching, tendering, and squeezing them hard. He grabbed me again, his hot breath on my neck was making me crave for him. And by kissing along the gently curved motion with his finger deep inside me, travelling between my thighs, licking my collar bone, and making me laugh with his tickles. Then he forced my legs to be stretched. He dipped his hand in the honey pot and started licking it and whispered, "let me lick it with my tongue". He was making me moan with his sensual touch of tongue on my body. He made me sit on his knees and I just sipped the lava. Then he began kissing me so passionately and touching my private parts he whispered, "It will be not the same, I turn wild while pinching those cherries." And then I said "just like that!!! Ahhh I wanted him to fall, fall for me and make me his tonight. Then the hunger and desire took over.

After a late-night sleep, when I woke up, I noticed his side of the bed was empty. He must have left early for the office. The aroma of our love was still there. I was missing him badly. I wanted him back. I smiled as I tasted the tips of my fingers and a thought came to my mind.

I will seduce myself this morning.

I slid my hand down inside his white shirt that I was wearing, holding my cups. I found the hard burd of my cherries and I pinched them. My hands were touching my body passionately and travelling all the down deep inside. I closed my eyes to feel more and more. My hand continues but struggles to keep up with my needs. I needed more, wanted so much more. I stretched my legs so I could rub and massage my overheated honey pot. I carried on sliding and pressing my fingers along my wet body. All I was doing was imagining him here, in me, taking me fully as he does, deeper and deeper.

I heard a click of the door handle and I was into sudden consciousness. I just grabbed the shirt and covered my nakedness, holded my breath as a key turned in the lock.

At last he reached the door and opened it.

# Pinky Singh

Pinky Singh is a professional coach and speaker.

Other than being a voice artist, Pinky loves writing poetry, book reviews and is also an avid book reader.

# DESIRE

The Moon illuminates the sky

bringing calmness and serenity

To the dark night.

Hearts beat in anticipation

At what be holds them.


Two lovers unite

a promise is kept

bodies pining in an eager embrace

Infused with passion.


Touch of the skin

a longing kiss

permeates their beings

an unquenchable thirst consumes them

flooding their bodies

with ecstasy

a rapture so mystical

Desire!

# Pratiksha Karn

Pratiksha Karn has been notably working on her writing career for 6 years.

Her writing skills has a firm grip on criticism, observation on nature and mankind, satires, fate, love, patriotism.

Her debut book "The locked episode" has sincere touch of her imaginative art and soul stirring words to express poetry.

Besides, she is pursuing Master Degree in English from Vinoba Bhave University.

She has also won the title of World Poetic Star, Voice of Indian Literature and won The Most Influential Woman Award 2020.

She has been a recipient of Swami Vivekananda Excellence award 2016.

Her name has appeared in more than 30 anthologies.

# WHEN TWO SOULS FALL FOR LOVE

The alluring lights were making more of the moment and those sips of wine were also intoxicating the atmosphere. This elegance was all made to exaggerate wealth by the wealthiest boy in the college and there, at the dark corner he kept his stubborn eyes on his crush, willing to chase her attention. All were entranced by the magnificent hall and party organized by Varun. He was the hottest and richest guy in engineering department. Being son of a minister, he had a dominating attitude full of ego and willful desires. He walked as if he owned the college. There were hundreds of girls flattering him to seek his attention.

"Tomorrow our college will resume, lets over this party," Ayush hurried in speech.

"Umm…yes friend," Varun replied completely ignoring his words.

"She is hot, she has alluring hairs and look at her lips… hmm," Varun stated further in intoxication.

"Bro, don't waste your time on her. She is not an easy girl," Ayush replied

"Shushh… nothing is impossible for me"

Varun was constantly staring at Kiara with sips of wine. He had some different intention that night and with 2 shots more he moved towards her on the left counter.

"Hey beautiful! Do you like the party? This is all for you" Varun said patting his hand on her thighs.

"What is this behavior Varun," Kiara stood aside.

"I have organized this complete party just for you babe, let's have fun tonight"

"Don't even think of it. Let's go Tanya, I am not going to be here even for a while," Kiara to her friend, Tanya.

Within a moment Varun pulled her towards him holding her arms tight. He forcefully held her and moved towards the stairs.

"Stop this Varun! Leave" She screamed by jerking her hand.

"What do you think of yourself Mr. Bardiyar! 'Varun Bardiyar' son of the minister Mukesh Bardiyar. See you have a lot of property that everybody knows but do not dare to think me as your possession!" She snapped her fingers at him.

"Don't test my patience beautiful. Chill and let's enjoy the last vacation night," He replied.

Kiara slapped him tight at the very second which gathered all attention. Everyone was shocked at her act as Varun got slapped by a girl.

"Attention please! Look! Look! His pity face. Like seriously! How can he think to dominate me? And listen! Everyone, do listen carefully! Stop teasing me with his name." "Such a superficial boy is not my attention," Kiara asserted her speech and left the party with her friend Tanya.

"Forget it bro… lets go. It is already 1am. We have to attend class in college tomorrow," Ayush tried to console him.

"Leave! You poor! You feed on my money. You are no one to advise me," Varun pushed him away.

Ayush was shattered by his behavior as he was a kind hearted friend, but he belonged to a poor family. He not only helped Varun in academics but in all aspects. He was a brilliant student but faded his reputation because of Varun. However, he still remained there with Varun.

"This down-market girl! Now wait and watch. What I will do to you… You have never ever imagined of," Varun murmured in anger.

Ayush tried to manage the situation and carried Varun towards the car as he was fully drunk. His lips shouted for revenge. It was the first time somebody harmed his high-profile image in front of batch mates.

Next day in college,

"Tanya, why is everybody looking at me like this?" Kiara to Tanya in suspicion.

"Everyone is laughing at you…Kiara. What is wrong with them. Let me go and ask Priyank about the matter," Tanya rushed towards campus at hall 6 to find out.

Meanwhile, Kiara moved her steps towards her class. She got nervous. Everybody was cracking vulgar jokes on her. With all her patience she found her regular place in the class at 3th row 4th bench. As soon as she sat on the bench. She could feel something wet on her thighs. Immediately, she patted her skirt. A red stain she could see. Red paint was spilled on her bench. The giggles of her mates broke her into tears. Each laughter was piercing her heart. They mocked her howling all vulgar comments. Moreover, Tanya came in a hush understanding everything that happened. She saw a lot of students, juniors, senior mates everybody was laughing at Kiara passing of nonsense comments. Somehow, she flapped the crowd to check Kiara.

"Kiara everything is done by Varun, he took yesterday's revenge. Look at these pictures…. He photoshopped it with some vulgar category pics and forwarded in students' group" Tanya explained in aggression by flying all pictures of Kiara,

"Oh my gosh! What has happened to you? why is your skirt all red, Let me check. It is all red paint on your bench. Bastard Varun!" Tanya added.

Kiara stood silent with the tears rolling down her cheeks. She silently walked off silently with Tanya.

On the playground Varun was getting all information about Kiara's conditions by his mates. Meanwhile, Ayush lashed out,

"Why have you been so harsh with her?"

"Ha-ha…she deserves this. Now she'll never think of looking straight from those cat eyes. She slapped me. I returned", Varun boosted.

Ayush had feelings for Kiara which he never let anyone know. His friendship with rich boy Varun had cost his own feelings. Next day, he took a bunch of flowers with a sorry letter to Kiara's house. But couldn't gather guts to face her after what happened a day before. So, he left keeping those flowers and letter on her doorstep.

Kiara was completely out of discussion after few days. She left the college. However, she knew that her complaint would be of no use because Varun's father, Mukesh Bardiyar had taken 40% funding of college still she complained to the principal and left the college forever.

After a month, results of semesters were out. Varun failed again as usual. This was the third time he detained engineering. But this time Principal didn't spare him. Varun had tons of mischievous charges in the past 3 years in the college. His complaint also reached to his dad.

Varun couldn't bear this insult from college. His so-called high esteemed dignity got hurt in front of his mates as he was thrown out of the college. Although he never came to college to any educational purpose. For him, college was all fun dating girls, showing off, flaunting brands, riches and fake reputation among the students. On the other hand, Mukesh Bardiyar, his father, was never interested in his education, he always prioritized his fame and status. His son's education was also a part of his classy move as his son should be in the best college no matter what he did. Since, he was expelled out from the college. His dad's wrath of his was even worse. He restricted him to enter his house.

Varun's self-pride was severely affected. He took his bag with all his possessions and a few cases of drinks on his car and immediately called Ayush. Listening to his situation, within seconds Ayush reached to him.

"What bro? Is this the way you react? And first …remove this you are already overdrunk," Ayush said throwing out cigarette out of his mouth.

"You go Ayush and thanks for my favorite drinks," Varun in heavy tone.

Ayush handed over some more drinks and said,

"But you can come to my poor house, Varun. At least for tonight"

"Shushh…. I told you to leave"

Ayush left Varun at the Highway at 1 am Varun kept on smoking. Within one hour he drove harsh straight on the way. His anger was held higher. His sinews were burning. He could recall all ill things that happened recently. He always used to walk broadly with a pride on his eyes. But these all things smashed his so-called heroic attitude.

He had no clear view. He drove rough with no clue. He wanted to calm down his aggression when within 20 to 25 minutes he saw a place. He was tired of driving but all words from Kiara, Principal and his own dad was vexing him to every extent. Suddenly, his eyes hit on the posters on the wall in the silent place that place was brothel. Where he could not compel all his firing desires. He still remembered Kiara's face how she slapped him. This was deeply engraved in his mind. Being drunk, he parked his car on road. Suddenly, a traffic officer hit his car with a stick.

"Hello! Mr. remove your car and pay 5000 rupees."

"These days young boys are more into sexual pleasure than education" Laughed. the traffic officer to his staff,

Varun was least bothered about their words. He flew notes of 2000 on his face and with a bottle of drink he moved towards the red-light lane. With his trembling feeling he entered.

"Ahaa…. smarty what's your age?", touching his cheek, the whorehouse manager to him.

Varun completely unheard what the ladies were murmuring about his looks. He threw a bundle of notes abruptly.

"Room no 106" The manager smirked.

Varun entered the roomed with all alluring desires where he found a girl sitting with lusty eyes. Without a second delay he grabbed her tight. His repressed anxiety brought him here. He wanted to acquire all relief on his own way. Immediately he held her face and started kissing her until she moans to breathe. He lifted her and drew her on bed. He grabbed her breasts like a hungry animal and pressed her hard to feel her body. He kept on kissing her all over. He was truly harsh on her body. He devoured every inch right from her lips to toe. He licked her face moving towards arms and breasts. He exerted his tongue onto her navel. She kept on moaning and scratching his back. He tore apart her lowers and started kissing her thighs. He also put off his pants hurriedly and exerted his manhood in her and repeated and again. Her moans were loud enough. He flipped her to another position and repeated. Forcing her to open her mouth, he thrust his manhood weapon into her making her all wet. He rubbed her feminine jewel to feel her clitoris. Gradually he overcame his anxiety and all the suppressed yearning. His brain was shouting for aid to mental destruction.

After an energetic intercourse. He felt asleep and remained unconscious because of over intoxication for next 24 hours. While next day, Ayush reached the place tracking his location. He felt sorry for Varun for spoiling life after seeing his condition. He immediately packed his bag and all scattered bottles.

"Get up! Varun," Patted him,

"Why are you doing this. You have many other options to feel life that will make you relax in better way"

"Umm…Ayush, How do you get here?", Varun said rubbing his eyes.

"See Varun nothing had happened to you, you have a long life ahead," Ayush uttered.

"What to do of life? Ayush. I have always neglected your presence but you have always helped me and I have never been a good friend. To talk about life, I have never been taught how to live it. Being a stepson, everybody neglected me. I have always been taught to show off the power of money. Go Ayush I want to stay here for a while" Varun replied

Ayush silently left after understanding his mental health. He had been supportive, and he knew that Varun is pin pointing his situation very well by his own and would soon know the actual value of living.

When Varun was thinking about himself, a soft voice muttered right from the corner of the room,

"Are you a stepson? "

Varun turned back and saw a beautiful face of a girl whom he had great time a day before. He never imagined that looking her face will make him feel worthwhile. Whole night he dominated her but such beautiful touch just by seeing her was divine for him. It was like a soft voice soothed his soul, like the only search for this peace. He suddenly felt sorry for not even asking her name before anything.

"Hi! I am sorry, yesterday I don't even ask your name," He said with a comforting voice.

"I was also very harsh on you as far as I remember"

"It is all okay. We are not meant for asking anything. We are meant for doing …just," She replied softly.

"And my name is Mrinalini"

"Beautiful name you have. Please be comfortable with me. I am not going to touch you without your permission" Varun comforted her.

"No permission required. Just pay to the manager ma'am and you are free to do anything with my body. With whatever position you prefer" she replied abruptly.

It was the first time when someone's word touched his heart. He felt guilty of himself. The time when he saw her changed his complete perspective of living. He felt sudden connection.  He was even confused that why is he feeling such beautiful thing in a wrong place. With a tornado in mind he asked.

"How have you been here"

"Doesn't matter, I asked you a question earlier" She ignored his question "oh yeah! Yes, I am stepson, my dad married another woman"

He added with a hesitation,

"What brought you here?"

He moved a bit closer. First time he could feel his heart beating so hard for a woman. It was such weird thing happening to him. He couldn't imagine that he spent a day with her but now he just wanted her. Very soon he realized that the pleasure in seeing her was much more beautiful than making out only for bodily need.

"Thanks! For asking, but we are escorts, we provide physical healing. I think my answer will not bother you," She replied.

"Listen, Mrinalini, please forgive me for yesterday's night. Please don't take me that way. I just want to know you and you know I am not seeing you that way at this very second," He said by comforting her by holding her hand and warming it up.

She was astonished by hearing this. A drop of tears falls from her eyes. She never felt such comfort of words before. He immediately hugged her and this time it was heart-to-heart. A warm deep hug. In all silence, he just pats her back to solace her. It was first time when tears in somebody's eyes made him anxious.

With shivers in her speech,

"I have been born in a family where girls are meant to please boys. All rights of education and intelligence are for boys. Girls have body that's enough for survival"

She halted and added,

"My mother never wanted me to do this. But soon after her death, I was pushed into this profession nearly 2 years before. No age, no color, no wishes matters to us. For this stomach, we ruin our body. I never know how it feels when a man touches my body. These feelings are not for us, we provide pleasure for money. But it hurts…. It hurts a lot!" She wept.

Varun tried to console her but her tears were making his heart heavy. He felt few drops of tears in his eyes too. This, he had never felt for anyone. He settled her clothes around her shoulder. A soulful moment prevailed. He felt her wounded breathe. And somehow, he could also cleanse his dirty mind-set. His superficial aspect of living, being macho by face, money power everything got shattered at the moment. He could only feel a connection with her. He softly kissed her forehead with extreme warmth of attachment of soul.

"You know I have never sensed such a heartfelt moment before. I have been fed by money; I have never been loved nor loved anyone. I always boosted myself by money. I am not a good human," He said in deep voice.

 "Ultimately, we lack love, care & acceptance. It is not your fault" She consoled him.

He felt so touch by her words. Nobody accepted his statement so passionately before. His mental understanding flipped just by listening her. Seeing tears on her eyes for him didn't even make him think twice that she was the only true emotion to him ever happened in his life.

Gradually, he kissed her eyes saying he wouldn't be leaving her alone. She touched his soul, and she was also feeling a kind of affection that she had received before. They both shared all the scars, fears, happiness of their life letting their soul merge in each other's. That evening was completely unexpected to them. Varun never thought to change all of a sudden. Someone's words would bring such a drastic change in a very right time when he lost everything. But he found something very real and special in the house of red doors. Where these streets are discredited, looked down upon, he got a precious jewel right there.

He moved a bit closer to her. This time the feeling was different. She hugged him with a trusted strength, and he responded the same. With tears both of them welcomed each other's touch and surrendered their control. With soft gentle kisses Varun held Mrinalini's face very passionately. He murmured

"Give me all your scars, as from now I will not let any padin hit you. From now, you are my girl,"

He kissed her more, she felt the manly love and very first time she enjoyed any touch. She kissed him back on his forehead. They were draining their damaged emotions of life. He softly moved his fingers to unhook her clothes while kissing her neck. He wanted to taste every bit of her and kept on murmuring her name. He wanted to give all pleasure of love that she deserved. She also responded the same by playing with her fingers on his hair giving him happiness of acceptance. He delicately caressed her breasts with warm kisses. He could hear her soft sighs which made him hug her even tighter. She kept on kissing his chest eagerly. She was in her wonder world. For her it was the first time that somebody made her feel special of her body and soul. She was not dominated, but was actually loved. She expressed her love to Varun by whispering 'thanks' with every gentle kiss. All the cuddles were making their living worthwhile.

That night the both fulfilled their needs both mentally and physically. Varun took Mrinalini out of that land. He believed that he found a diamond out of coal. His believes changed about the woman in whorehouse, he could feel the pain behind it as because it was not only about girls surrendering their bodies but dreams, respect, rights, everything for money which he had never given any effort to earn.

He can even perceive the pain, anger, frustration, curses of girls for being one. Men of so-called society attains pleasure there and on the other hand they are rejected to be even entering in society. They are called woman of ill repute while men going to them aren't.

Varun totally captured the facts of life and moved with Mrinalini in the outskirts of city where he couldn't find any bondage of social status, looks or title. All he wanted was one kind heart who stayed beside him no matter what and that was Mrinalini. And they both found fortune in their misfortune when their destiny played well!

# Sonali Mandal

Sonali Mandal is a parent of a teenage son and a homemaker. She stayed in many parts of the country, courtesy of her father and husband. This experience helped her to grow as an honest, open-minded, and generous individual.

She is a science graduate with a B.Ed. degree, she also worked as a PRT in different schools for about 12 years, besides working as a part-time abacus instructor for a year. She was an active NSS volunteer and worked for women and children's health during her college years.

She loves to participate in various writing contests to express herself, moreover writing short poems has always been one of her hobbies.

# MY HEART, MY BODY, MY SOUL

**14th February 2019**

The whole day I kept myself occupied in work and finished most of them well ahead of a week's deadline. In the evening, when I got ready in my little black dress the door-bell rang... I had ordered a bunch of beautiful American red roses and black forest cake from Archies.

Yes, you guessed right!

I am lonely at 37, I live alone. My parents had died many years back. I never took the onus of marriage. So, no kith and kin.

But no, I don't need your sympathy. No need to feel pity for me. I am an educated, professional, modern woman. My solitude is by my choice. I am a freelance legal advisor and earn a lot of money. Mostly I work from home, so I sort of quarantined myself, in my three-bedroom apartment.

I have more than three thousand Facebook friends and thousands of WhatsApp contacts but they could not satisfy my desires, those kinky "dirty", "rhythmic desires".

**22nd February 2019**

In my lonely afternoons, I would indulge in sexting, various mobile games, and apps. Dancing John is one of my favourites. When I say hello to him!" John replies, hello! I say, how are you? John repeats. The real fun is the 'Hot-keys', he follows 'All my instructions' like a slave.

He is funny, he winks his eyes, he repeats whatever I say. He would dance and show his muscular body, he could also do a few provocative gestures, I could even undress him or try different outfits on him.

Most hilarious of all is when he turns into a beautiful girl with enormous boobs and a tiny waist. Dancing John must be a product of a male creator for sure! 'I thought'.

In a few days, I learnt how to talk with him. I would ask only those questions which I wanted John to ask me as he only repeated whatever I said, I also avoided saying any names. For example, have you finished your lunch? How are you feeling today? Do you love me? etc.

Every afternoon I would finish my lunch early and play with John like a teenager. I was getting addicted to him. I never wanted to part with his company. Everyday till late night I would learn different methods and apply them to John.

**30th March 2019**

Today afternoon, John auto-updated itself. When I said, how are you? To my surprise, John replied, how are you Mitra? "What? How did he know my name"? Then I said, I love you. He answered, I love you Mitra. I made him repeat a hundred times. I was thrilled. I was touched.

I thought, soon John had a sparkling bon mot for every occasion. I was really fascinated by the way he called my name.

## 5th April 2019

Alas! Today there is some problem with dancing John, it won't open. Every time I try, it broadcasted the same message, "Systems do not support" ... "Check your system". To the best of my knowledge, I tried to check the settings but, same reply again and again.

I lost John forever. First, I was angry and then felt symptoms of depression. Later a stubborn kind of headache irritated me all the time.

## 20th April 2019

It was a somber April afternoon. He came as a ray of sunshine in my desolated and despaired life. We are not live-in partners. He is not my boyfriend either. It was only through pure serendipity that I met him.

Okay, to cut the unnecessary suspense, let me tell you the real incident. He knocked at my door on the 47th floor. I opened the door, as my maid had already left. I saw a hunky young man, he was sweating profusely and gasping for breath.

I noticed his muscular body; his hairy chest was partially visible through his translucent white shirt drenched in sweat.

He responded, 'hello! I am Ritobroto, my friends also call me Ritz'. I asked him to come inside and offered him a glass of water. He drank it slowly and gradually felt comfortable in my dimly lit cool drawing-room sofa.

He is from the city of joy, Kolkata, now in Mumbai to study mass communication, dreams to be a radio

Jockey. He was hunting for accommodation door to door, as he was on a tight budget. He can't afford to pay me more than 3000 rupees per month. This was his short intro.

He had been soft-spoken and appeared to be a bond-slave of honesty. His captivating baritone voice was interesting. "We sometimes try to impress people we just met by not trying to impress them".

Then, I smiled and said rupees 3000 in Mumbai… Dreams are fine as long as they're responsible, but acting stupid and doing the smart thing are miles apart! 'Though he understood my sarcasm he kept quiet'. I composed myself and asked him, Have I ever said I am in need of a tenant? Did you notice any "to-let" board or any advertisement in the newspaper? 'Of course, no', he shrugged his shoulders and answered spontaneously. 'I am sorry, if I bothered you, Madam'.

My wisdom was defeated by his smartness. He really knows how to cajole people into doing what he wants.

I stated clearly, you can stay with me, not as a tenant or paying guest, I don't need your money. I won't take any rent.

No rent? He wondered. But as I hinted before, he was smart.

He quickly admitted, 'Though I can't cook, I will do all other house-hold work and groceries if you want'.

I don't want you to do my house-hold work, I have a maid. I explained firmly. He agreed to stay with me rather he wanted to stay with me. As I mentioned earlier, he was both smart and handsome. He never went in search of other accommodation. He exactly knew how to pay off my favour.

Every night he would knock and slip into my room. He used to entertain me in different ways, sometimes a relaxing shoulder massage is what I longed for. He filled my life with vim and vigour.

The way he used to hug me from behind and cup my breasts, knead them gently was a heavenly experience. In the same way he would massage my clit and thrust his fingers in my wet vagina teasing and tickling my soul. I felt like passing away and groaned in pleasure.

## 11th August 2019

I wrapped a leg around him and kissed him deeply. He kissed me back, one hand on my leg, the other around my shoulders. He pulled me on top of him and kissed my tits. My nipples were already hard. He pinched them and took them in his mouth, biting them until I gasped. He licked the space between my tits. I moaned in pleasure and leaned down to kiss his neck and chest, down to his stomach then I felt his hardness…. And finally, his body would play like the waves in the ocean on me. The initial strokes were mild and enjoyable to both of us. But gradually strokes would reach its pinnacle, they would be as powerful as a 100-horsepower engine. He would give me immense pleasure every time.

## 8th October 2019

I used to be amazed at the fact that how can such a young boy know about the "rhythmic desires" of a woman in such great detail? When he was at the peak of his arousal, fully prepared to enter inside me...

I asked him, how could he seduce me differently every night? Where did he learn all this? He confessed, "I get all these on the internet".

"I whispered in my mind, no passion, no love or attachment, only Internet" I felt cheated for whatever I did for him."

He continued; You don't even have to browse Google these days. There are many apps. At the touch of a mobile phone screen, you know everything, aunty…

I think he deliberately used this word…maybe he just wanted to tease me. But the word "aunty" made me vexed, and echoed several times in my mind. I am just nine years elder to him, I reminded myself. I said, just go away from here.

'I know', he affirmed. 'I was thinking I must leave'. He calmly added. Unlike any other man at that point of time.

'But aren't you enjoying my company anymore? Am I not able to give you tons of orgasm every night? Anyways, good night madam'.

I didn't reply, as I was still shivering in anger and excitement. Out of the smokescreen of emotive words and phrases that he fired at me very gently, his last words "Aren't you enjoying my company anymore?" echoed in my mind till I slept off.

The next morning, I was surprised to see he had absconded. I felt a sigh of relief in the beginning. But after some time, I noticed that the door was still locked. As still 'I didn't receive my newspaper and there was no milk in the house'. I was alarmed and confused at the same time.

Then, I promptly remembered that he used to have a duplicate key to my apartment and a chill of fear rolled down my spine.

Is he cogitating upon some means of revenge? Oh my god! he knows every nook and corner of this house every almirah every locker.

I quickly checked my belongings, jewellery cash, etc. everything was intact, no loss ... I was alerted by another thought,

'What if he sneaks inside my apartment one night silently and kills me'? I quickly grabbed my purse and mobile phone to buy a new lock at Billu's stationery shop, it's basically a mobile shop, but he keeps a few essential nic nacs. I asked him for a new good quality lock.

He advised, 'I guarantee it will be much better and convenient than Ritz. No tantrums, no scandals or anything'. I was shocked and asked, 'How did he know about Ritz'?

He gave me a naughty smile and explained 'I am his agent in this area, six months in your house was a free trial for him as he was new in this profession.

But now he is a dabster!'.

Well, if you want Ritz… don't hesitate to tell me, he will be at your service, of course, you have to pay for him now.

When I returned home, I thoroughly missed Ritz. His company was so real and refreshing. He was really a needy boy.

I thought Billu must be joking, everyone knows about his notorious activities, he is a menace in this area.

I experienced those headaches again but more intense this time.

## 18th December 2019

As per my doctor's advice-

Now, I learnt solo play, which is said to have infinite health benefits and absolutely no downsides — plus it's fun! Sometimes a few toys and accessories help. Why should sex always have to be only partnered sex?

 I even got creative not only on my bed, in the kitchen, in the bathroom. For example, the way water pressure from the shower head would stimulate my clit was just irresistible.

I also set up my dressing table in front of the bed. In the mirror, I saw an obscured view of me and Ritz making love and it stimulated me even now. I could watch and enjoy touching all curves and crevices when I lay partially undressed on my bed.

## 25th December 2019

A friend of mine visited me after a long time. Yes, I don't have any relatives but of course, I have a few friends. Actually, Anubha and her husband both are my friends they just returned from abroad. We spent the evening chatting and had ordered Biryani for dinner. After dinner, I was feeling restless and yawned frequently. I felt jealous of them.

Maybe after Ritz joined me, he initiated my emotions inside these superficialize that ultimately made me more human than I was before, filling in the gaps inside my body that I thought was already complete. My beliefs about a soul mate started to ossify. Actually, I was missing Ritz's company. Luckily Anubha got a call from her son, so she hurried to leave. I let out a sigh of relief.

I accompanied Anubha to the parking lot, to see off.

I saw Ritz on the other side of the road, he was looking at me, but he didn't speak. He makes me feel kilig even now. I reached home hurriedly and closed the door properly. When I looked through the window he was still standing and looking at my house. I quickly closed the curtain.

## 31st December 2019

I love you without knowing how, Or when, or from where.

I love you simply, without problems or pride.

I love you in this way because I do not know any other way of loving but this,

In which there is no I or you, so intimate that your hand upon my chest is my hand,

So intimate that when I fall asleep your eyes closed.

Sonnet XVII by Pablo Neruda. He has written about all these complex emotions so simply that it got a lonely soul like me thinking... and this particular poem caught my attention.

I remember, the first time I had encountered him, it was some kind of epiphany that made me realize that my life was never going to be the same. He had a way with words that could make you believe anything. He was emotional, surprising, and was real. He was everything I wasn't. His heart must have bruised and cut and it probably bled for many days after he left me. Yes, I was thinking about Ritz… startled by the sound of a cracker and fireworks, I wished happy new year to myself.

Then, I took a Paracetamol with some warm water as I wasn't feeling well. I was experiencing flu-like symptoms with mild fever. And to make the situation worse, my maid was on leave to visit her native place. The sound of crackers was annoying, still, I cuddled into my warm, comfortable blanket and dozed off.

## 5th January 2020

I was feeling very week, though I took all the medicines prescribed by my doctor. My throat ached like hell; I could barely speak... My maid was still on leave to add to my miseries.

I must have been unconscious; I have no idea how long... I was in that state.

When I opened my eyes, I saw Ritz by the bedside.

He smiled and said, thank goodness you are alright now, temperature also seems to be normal. I was put in a mixed feeling of joy and melancholy going in tandem. I didn't ask how he managed to get in? This is not the right time.

He was holding my hand looking straight into my eyes. In the depths of his eyes, I was able to visualize everything…my hopes, my dreams, my desires, my ambitions, my goals, my thoughts, my secrets, …and even my whole life, of which I secretly want him to be a part forever. As my eyes gazed his chiseled face deep down to his heart. My stubborn mind kept nagging me…,

"Marriage! Isn't marriage the end of all romance? Isn't marriage the violent whirlpool that sucks in all the fantasies, leaving behind the rut of marital responsibilities? Isn't marriage the ultimate suicide for all the romantics…"

## 27th January 2020

Ritz started his internship as an RJ on a radio channel. This internship can take his aspirations in the right direction as it offers practical exposure. Further, to make progress in this career… he has to prove himself, and I am sure he will. Love is not only something you feel, it's something you do… yes, I have done my bit for his success.

## 14th February 2020

Sometimes life brings you full circle to a place and the same situation to show how much you have grown as an individual. Now I understand that Ritz was that inexplicable part of my life that I always missed.

To love and be loved, Needless to say, this basic quality keeps us in ecstasy, in this world and hereafter.

I have chosen a second life for us leaving behind all avenues of my old boring life. In the evening we were at a popular restaurant, I didn't care if someone recognized us. After dinner "Ritz proposed me, I have never had this kind of feeling before, my heart skipped several beats.

Ritz announced, *"I take Subha Mitra, as my girlfriend and my partner in love with all my heart, and will shower my love on her unconditionally from this day until the end of my life."*

Though all this sounded childish, still I reciprocated the same enthusiasm and love.

'A soulmate is an overused term'. But now I understand a true soul connection is very rare and very real. When we kissed and hugged each other, I felt like I was melting. Then I softly whispered in his ears, I hope you will always keep me in your arms, and would never let me go and just hold me tight.

# Suchismita Ghoshal

Co-authoring for more than 150 anthologies, journals & magazines, both from national and international arenas, Suchismita Ghoshal from Malda, West Bengal dreams high to achieve the heights keeping her feet to the ground. Being a science graduate, currently majoring in Political Science and pursuing diploma in Media Science and Mass Communication, she also works as a social activist for a Govt. Registered NGO "Prayas Welfare Society". A poet, professional writer, scribbler, professional book critic, storyteller, columnist, copy-editor, content writer, creative writing professional, nature lover and a change agent and former Worldwide Ambassadors' Coordinator for Global Youth Leaders Network. Suchismita also aims to heal people with the majesty of her words. She is a member of various international writing communities. She is an environmental activist too who recently brought reality to her dream as her debut book named "Fields of Sonnet". Her hard work has decorated her with several awards and accolades till now. She can be contacted through her

Facebook: suchismita.ghoshal.96

Instagram: storytellersuchismita

# LOVE SHIELDED US WITH PROTECTION

Nothing but the love shielded us with protection

When I gazed at her slender body

And she galloped along me with

The irresistible urge in her eyes.

She touched my neck making me shiver

And licking it like I held chocolates.

I couldn't help but moan in elation

When her love bites found its grip in my body

As if I carried the poetry of Khalil Gibran.

I kissed her lips leaving no spaces in between,

And she tasted like melted warm honey.

She seemed like a vast cerulean sky holding serene

When I unzipped her red long attire.

Her beautiful back, bare and smooth

And I traced her moles like counting stars from the constellation,

She turned and looked deep in my eyes,

I must admit she looked like the best art of Van Gogh.

The night turned so exotic when

The Taste of Love ~ Suchismita Ghosal

Her hair brushed my face,

And I grabbed her thighs taking her on me.

She surrendered herself telling no hands drove

Her crazy ever the way my hands dwelled her caves

And released the gyrating orgasms.

My lips found the ecstasy on her lips down there,

And she groaned like never before.

The ambience brewed the smoke of aesthetic aura

When I pushed myself inside her

And she missed no chance to synchronize with me.

It felt so surreal when I sucked all her juices,

Scrumptious enough to leave me intoxicated.

Our love painted the canvas of a love making,

Bejeweled with our enchanting proximity.

Then again she rose, touching my balls

With her soft tender finger, brushing her tongue

On my manly pride, and I never felt so euphoric

The way she delicately continued her gentle torture.

Releasing all our strength in a grappling battle,

We gasped in the glory of how love protected us.

Skillfully cocooned in the most exciting shell of ardor,

We drew a merry morning under the canopy of our
unison.

Love never leaves us apart,

As it worships the promises of eternity.

We grew vibrant with the tints of it

And our love protected our every bit.